Three Beautiful Ways
to Move Forward in Life

Padma Jyoti **Dr. G. S. Ayyappan**

Three Beautiful Ways to Move Forward in Life
Dr. G. S. Ayyappan
First Published: August, 2024
Published by

INDIAN UNIVERSITIES PRESS
Imprint of Bharathi Puthakalayam
7, Elango Salai, Teynampet, Chennai - 600 018
044 -24332424, 24332924, 24330024
Email: bharathiputhakalam@gmail.com | www.thamizhbooks.com

Rs.50/-
Printed at Printech, Chennai - 600 005.

Preface

"This book was written to show the value of time for everyone who is wasting time and worrying about not being able to achieve the goal on time."

The book titled "Three Beautiful Ways to Move Forward in Life", very clearly speaks about the 'self-realization', 'time management' and 'leadership quality' required to make progress in life so that anyone can adapt in their life.

The author has designed this book in such a way that it can be easily followed by combining the instructions for becoming an achiever with day-to-day activities. Through this book, the author emphasizes that there is nothing that cannot be achieved without self-confidence and perseverance.

It's great to describe a story about 100% success through planning, preparing, and then execution, under the title of time management. It is the specialty of the author to lay down five principles: planning, setting priorities, setting realistic goals & deadlines, avoiding distraction & laziness, and smart work instead of hard work.

This book was well written to show the value of time for everyone who is wasting time and worrying about not being able to achieve the goal on time. Dear readers, kindly read this book, which asserts that you can overcome the waste of time, break down the barriers in life and achieve your goal.

Let's turn our lives into a book that others love to read. Best wishes for your well-being.

Dr. A. Robert Sam
Writer, Senior Principal Scientist,CSIR-CSIO Chennai

Greetings

"The author of the book asserts that if there is one thing that everyone should learn, feel and practice in life, it is time management."

My dear readers who consider reading to be the breath of life! Book lovers! First of all, my heartfelt salutations to you all. I am very much delighted to congratulate People's Scientist, Padma Jyoti, Dr. G.S. Ayyappan on his sixth book titled "Three Beautiful Ways to Move Forward in Life". My gratitude to the author and the publisher of the book for providing such an opportunity.

There is no doubt that this book will be a guiding light not only for the student community but also for all mankind who want to succeed and achieve. The specialty of the author of this book is that he gives quotes and examples in the simplest way possible, practically, with short stories, to make it easier to understand. The author has implemented the same in this book as well.

The uniqueness of this book is that it summarizes in a simple way the views of many successful achievers and the methods followed by them. Thiruvalluvar, a famous Tamil Poet who wrote Thirukkural says that "Saying is simple to anyone – but following the same is difficult in life" and "The best Word in the World is Action" and the part that indicates that you should be acting rather than being the word warriors is very wonderful.

Titled "Self-Realisation", the first way to move forward, it is wonderful to have a clear and elegant grasp of how important confidence and self-confidence are to succeed in life. Similarly, it is good to describe faith in three different ways. The author's poem on the topic of self-confidence also sows an upsurge in the thoughts of the reader. The tips he gives to build self-confidence are superb.

The second pathway is entitled "Time Management". Starting with the aptest proverbs such as "Time is like gold; Duty is like the eye", "Sprinkle when there is Wind", and "Cultivate in Time", it is wonderful to explain the five principles of adhering to time management. I also liked "deciding priorities". The author of the book asserts that if there is one thing that everyone should learn, feel and practice in life, it is time management.

As the third pathway, the author has become himself as a leader; described under the title "Leadership". It is wonderful to describe the barriers and the qualifications to become a leader, as the first obstacle to becoming a leader is the habit of blaming others by naturally saying "Kallu Idichiruchi, Mullu Kuthiruchi". Kalam's story is a great example of that. I urge you to imbibe what is said in this book, inculcate it in your mind as a nail put on the fresh tree, follow suit in life, and wish you all the best to achieve and move forward and read a lot of such thoughtful books. I wish the author of the book to write up to hundreds of books and benefit many without stopping at these four.

Yours faithfully,
Mrs. N. Sangeetha
Home Manager, Social Reformer, Chennai

Foreword

Dear readers who feel reading books is breath and lives! Dear friends! Who admires the book as intellectual property! Proud Gentlemen! My dear respected Students! And Children! The title of this book I wrote is "Three Beautiful Ways to Move Forward" in the hope that you would read a lot of books with the sincere aim of progressing in life. Yes, there are numerous ways to succeed and advance in life, but in this book, I've categorized them into three categories that are both very clear and easy to understand.

The specialty of Tamil is its "Numbers and Letters". In that sense, I have described the significance of the number in the book "This is How I Won – The Secret of Success". I have also explained the significance of numbers three, five, nine, eighteen, twenty-seven, etc in that book. With that in mind, I have tried to highlight the significance of number three in this book and show the three most important ways to move forward in life.

In the first chapter, I have started with a short explanation, stating the three beautiful ways to move forward as a brief introduction;

- Self-Realization,

- Time Management, and

- Leadership Quality

In the second chapter of the book, the first pathway forward I dealt with is "self-realization". In this topic, I have explained about self-confidence, and how important self-realization is. "If you think you can. It will happen". Yes. I have shared some of the stories as an example of what I had read on the website. To make it more interesting I have shared a few stories too.

In the third chapter, I mentioned about "time management" as the second pathway to progress. Starting with the lovely Tamil proverbs, "Kaalam Pon Pondrathu; Kadamai Kan Pondrathu" which means "Time is like Gold; Duty is like the Eye", "Kaatrullapothe Thootrikkol" which means "Sprinkle when there is wind". In this chapter, I have described how important time management is to move forward in life.

In Chapter 4, I have explained "Leadership" as the third pathway to progress. Yes, I've also mentioned how crucial leadership is to succeed and victory. I explained in a very straight forward manner the stages necessary for taking on leadership responsibilities from the classroom to parliament. "Leader! Or Follower! I have also narrated a true incident that happened in the life of the People's President, Dr. A.P.J. Abdul Kalam.

In chapter 5, I have explained not as a conclusion, but as a starting point for conquering barriers. I have stated not as a series of advice, but as suggestions, on what barriers must be broken to succeed in life like a Karuthu Kandhasamy. I have documented what I know, including how to turn failures into successes, how to make life experiments successful, your economic status is not a hindrance at all, and that success is assured if ignorance and superstition are eliminated.

There is a Thirukkural in Valluvan's thoughts when he says, "To say is simple to anyone - to act as it is said". It's easy for anyone to comment. However, I feel I am fit to say as I have implemented the same and achieved it; and also writing them as a book. At this point, I am reminded of a dialogue that appeared in a movie – "Ulagin Thalai Sirantha Sol; Seyal" which means "The best word in the world is the Action". Really how true it is!

The ideas presented in this book should be internalized, nurtured, and felt by every reader and student. The intention of this book is that "You must Succeed". It wouldn't be an overstatement to claim that I've read a lot of books that have helped me to become a successful person. I will be privileged and feel proud if you believe that this book helped you to recognize who you are and inspired you to stand up in life, just as it did for me. I, the book's author, will also be satisfied. In the same way that you have supported all of my previous publications, I would like to request you render the best support for this one as well.

Ever Yours – People's Scientist
Dr. G.S. Ayyappan

Contents

Chapter-1
Three Ways to Move Forward

Every successful person in this world who has succeeded looks back on their journey at some point. It will frequently be a hardroute. Everybody who has attained the highest level of achievement has gone through numerous strikes and trials in life, but it is the outcome of doing it voluntarily. Eventhough there are several methods to win, these are the three that the majority of winners mention for the reason of success.

Here are three ways to move forward:

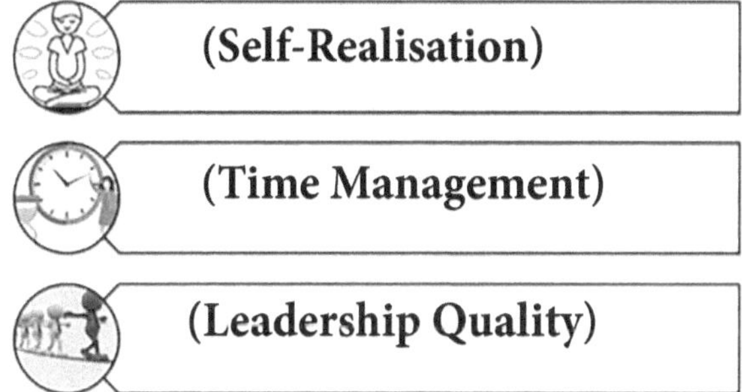

Self-Realization:

The first pathway to progress in life is self-realization. The first step towards self-realization is confidence and self-confidence. "Think I can; It will happen". Confidence or Faith is believing someone; Yes, it is good; but, Self-Confidence is more powerful than anything else. More preciously and accurately, Self-Confidence can be defined as believing in ourselves. Only when you believe someone then only you will be believed by others.

Confidence can be divided into three categories; Poor-Confidence, Over-Confidence, and Self-Confidence. If someone says "I CAN NOT DO it or I Don't KNOW ANYTHING"; that reflects their Poor Confidence. If you say that "I CAN ONLY DO it or I KNOW EVERYTHING", that reflects your Over Confidence. The people who say "I CAN DO IT and I KNOW SOMETHING"; reflect their Self Confidence. There are many strategies to increase your self-confidence. One of them is self-realization. In Chapter 2, we will discuss in more detail how self-determination or realization enables us to move forward and succeed in life.

Time Management:

Let me present "time management" as the second pathway of progress. I hope you too agree with this. Starting with the lovely Tamil proverbs, "Kaalam Pon Pondrathu; Kadamai Kan Pondrathu" which means "Time is like Gold; Duty is like the Eye", "Kaatrullapo the Thootrikkol" which means "Sprinkle when there is wind".

Under the sub-title "Gift Offered by God", some people always say that "There is no time; I don't have enough time; but how it is possible for you; and how you are managing". For them, I have described how I accomplish it. There is a saying that "Fools would have learned by their own experience, but wise people learn from others' experiences". I've also discussed under the title "Rectification of Wrongs" in keeping with the proverb "the wise man will learn a lesson from the surroundings and repent".

I've also outlined five fundamental principles that you should follow if you wish to become more adept at time management. Like the Panchsheel principles model, I have mentioned the need for planning, choosing priorities, setting realistic objectives and deadlines, staying focused and eschewing distractions, and smart work rather hard work. You may enjoy the brief story I told you as Ayyappananda, as a follower of Swami Vivekananda. "Hard Work Never Fails, but Smart work ever Succeed".

Leadership Quality:

I'm not the only one who believes that leadership is the third path to success; many others do as well. Yes, everyone is aware of how crucial leadership is if one wants to succeed. I have outlined the steps necessary to fulfill the responsibility of leadership, i.e., leader from school to parliament, in chapter 4 in a very straight forward manner.

"Leaders! Or Followers! If one learns about the qualities required to become a leader such as patience, simplicity, duty, clarity, knowledge, wisdom, etc., one can become a great leader. In particular, it is said that Karmaveera Kamarajar is a great leader. How did he get the title of "Perunthalaivar"? Is it not surprising that it was his wonderful qualities of him that made him a great leader?

We must cultivate the beautiful trait of not blaming people in particular. We will succeed if we are aware of and adhere to the actual event that gave rise to the people's president and Missile Man, Dr. A.P.J. Abdul Kalam, which was a very important quality to become a great leader. Dear readers! Are you prepared to comprehend your situation once you are aware of the first of the three possible paths forward—"self-realization"?

Chapter – 2
Self-Realization

Out of the three paths forward, let's start exploring the first path "self-realization." Let us learn about self-actualization's significance in fostering self-confidence in this topic. Using the saying "If you think it can be done, it will happen" as an example, I'll share with you some intriguing facts and anecdotes that I have read on the internet. I am ready. Are you ready?

Self-realization:

The term "self-realization" refers to the realization of one's own special traits and inner potential. Confidence and Self Confidence are the two hands for success. No matter how others describe confidence and self-confidence, I define myself in a different way. Yes "My way, a unique way."

Belief or Faith:

The Tamil proverbs "Faith does not perish", "Faith is life", and "Believe yourself" affirm this. First of all, we can understand not only what faith is but also how to succeed and travel the path of faith or belief.

It is impossible to succeed in life without faith. There is faith or belief in God for the atheist; faith itself is God for others. That is the distinction, but the reality is that matter cannot exist without faith.

An idea that originated in the mind of one of the Tamil writers Ilamathi is depicted here. The fish and parrot are captives in their tanks, unable to free themselves or even attempt to escape; they are victims of their circumstances, much as a robber under the control of the law can break out from prison.

Not everyone tries to run away which has the fifth sense. While experiences are not shared equally and faith is a question of personal conviction, all humans are created equally and capable of achieving what is intended. Because of faith, the incorrect man's effort is a transient success. Will our good efforts fail when faith encourages misguided efforts? When you accept acceptable needs, it has to be extremely successful. How could a lofty aspiration be wasted? Should we fail, it could be due to improper effort or, more likely, a lack of confidence in our abilities. We must always keep in mind the concept of Ilamathi throughout our life.

Alexander the Great is the first person who springs to mind when discussing heroes. When Alexander the Great's army was losing ground in a war that was raging through Greece and defeat was approaching him unexpectedly, his commander, remarked, "Oh King! The enemy has more than one lakh soldiers, but we have only half of them. Hence it is very difficult to defeat in the war". With a giggle, the hero Alexander exclaimed, "What a Commander! I think you forgot me. Include me as well. This force will do. Prepare and be ready for the war." This conversation shows his conviction that he possesses the same bravery as fifty thousand people. Yes. That is the belief. Confidence.

The kitchen, bedroom, and bathroom are essential components of every house, and we need to know what, when, and how much importance to give each one. Furthermore, the faith we place in others determines whether our activities are successful, so it's critical to recognize this.

Swamy Vivekananda said dared and boldly that "Give me a hundred energetic and active youths, and I will transform India". Therewere two reasons for his bold and daring comments. Vivekananda's belief in the youth is the first. Secondly, the conviction that India is capable of changing.

Similarly, the People's President, A.P.J. Abdul Kalam declared that "Give me thousands of dignified Students; I will make this India a Strengthen and developed country. Afterwards neither God nor devil can change them". Kalam had a strong faith in the student community.

Faith is extremely necessary for the nation and the individual. Life is always a paradise for those who have mastered the thought that they can, and a desert for those who hold superstitious ideas that they cannot. They claim it will happen when theythink I can.

A teacher ought to have faith in his pupils. Every student ought to have faith in their instructors. Every parent ought to have faith in their kids. All children ought to have faith in their parents. A husband must have faith in his spouse and vice-versa. It is existence. Indeed, life is faith.

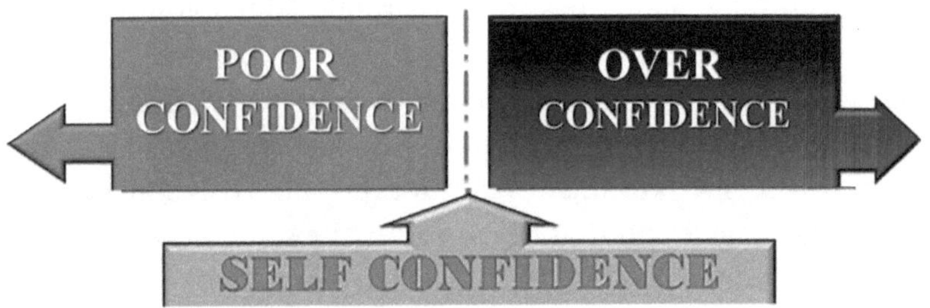

Confidence or faith can be divided into three categories; Poor-Confidence, Over-Confidence, and Self-Confidence. If someone says "I CAN NOT DO it or I Don't KNOW ANYTHING"; that reflects their Poor Confidence. If you say that "I CAN ONLY DO it or I KNOW EVERYTHING", that reflects your Over Confidence. The people who say "I CAN DO IT and I KNOW SOMETHING"; reflecttheir Self Confidence. The "I can do it" mindset is a sign of self-confidence.

Self-confidence:

Believing in oneself is the foundation of confidence, which is the awareness of our unique abilities. Put another way, self-confidence stems from an understanding of one's abilities and qualities. The first step towards progress in life is self-realization, which can be achieved in several ways, one of which is the realization of self-realization.

Faith is useful. Self-confidence is growing stronger. Self-confidence can only grow when one feels self-assured; and when self-confidence grows, success is guaranteed no matter what one does. Self-confidence is equivalent to the strength of 10 elephants if faith is comparable to the strength of an elephant. This poetry, which I wrote on confidence, is available on the website.

Self-confident

My dear Friend! My sweet young man!
"Know yourself. You will know yourself"
This is the philosophy of the Greek sage.

"If you know yourself – if you know yourself,
you can live in the world – you can rule this world,"
This is the philosophical song of the Tamil poet.

This is an attempt...

An attempt to open the doors of locked thoughts!
A revolution that awakens a sleeping young man!
This poet, scattered in my field of thought, is also a witness!
You are awake, my friend... You win - that's the joy!

The victory is yours...

"My friend! Tomorrow's is ours," said one of the poets!
Tomorrow is not ours, but today is
what we say in the hands of the young man!
"Young man, get up, wake up!
Work until you take away your success!
The victory is yours... The victory is yours!

Why this reluctance?

Aa... Young man, are you afraid?
What are you afraid of?
Are you looking for something somewhere?
Have you lost something?
What are you looking for?
Where are you looking?
You're looking for something that's within you!
But searching it outside – Why this reluctance?

You Can...

You can! You can! You can only!
This is the trust I have in you!
I can... I can... You tell me that!
It's the confidence you have in yourself!

Who is he?

Everyone has a close friend in his life!
A wonderful companion who is frozen within you!
A magician who burns memories and
makes dreams come true - who is he?

A Crutch...

A crutch that makes you feel!
A trick that changes one's self!
The magic wand that adds several crowns!
Success... Success... Victory over victory!
- a scepter that you hold to swear!
That's the hope!
Self-confidence! Self-confidence!

Confidence - Self-confidence...

I can't- I can't do anything, I can't do anything!
That is Poor Confidence!
If I say you can! you can! you can do it!
That is Confidence!
I can! I can Do it! I can too!
That is Self-confidence!

In conclusion...

My dear friend!
It is your dream - the dream of your Nation!
It's your effort - the rise of your Country!
It's in your victory! Our Victory!
It's your future - the dawn of the motherland!
It's enough to sleep - wake up - come on, my friend!
Let us make our nation a prosperous and proud country!
Always shoulder to shoulder for you!

Let me now put forward a question that some people ask me. "How to develop self-confidence? How do we know if one is self-confident?" Let us now look at the qualities required to develop self-confidence within a person.

Assertiveness: You must learn to stand in front of yourself and persevere until you finish whatever activity you take on. This applies to anything you undertake. Success in life is assured if you have a strong reputation and hold Bharathiyar's song firmly in your mind – ManathilUruthiVendum.

Optimism: Whatever you do, you must remain impartial toward everything and possess confidence in everything. If you possess this one trait, your confidence will shine through.

Eagerness: There needs to be initiative to create self-confidence. Success is certain if you work hard and do everything sincerely and heartfelt with eagerness We refer to that as egoism.

Affection or Attachment: Self-sufficient People possess a strong sense of enthusiasm for their nation, society, family, and themselves. They also exhibit a certain level of affection and fondness for their friends. Passion and attachment are two distinct things.

Pride: Confident people always have a positive self-image. To think otherwise is a matter of pride rather than headgear. You'll look at yourself and think, "I'm all a vest," if you look at some people,they would degrade themselves by saying, "I don't have the slightest talent". Self-Confident people say "Nothing is wrong" and even if something failed, then one should say "I don't mind. Let's learn from our failure experience in the future". When something is completed successfully and satisfactorily, "Excellent. Shake things up. "Sabash" is how you have to lift your spirits. You need to feel good about yourself. I used to pull my shirt collar and say "Sabash" to myself whenever I was on stage or attending an event as a distinguished guest. This is one way of self-motivating. This will help us feel more confident in ourselves.

Independence: Freedom is something that should not be misconstrued. Saying "freedom" does not imply moral transgressions in one's attire or the pursuit of civilization. Individual freedoms include the ability to write, speak, think, act, and make decisions. They also include the development of self-confidence.

Trust: As previously stated, we must believe in something, and we must believe that faith is life. Only when we have faith in other people can we gain their belief, which in turn will boost our confidence.

Ability to handle Criticism–Acceptance ofAccusations: Not everyone has this mindset. When someone points out anything we did incorrectly, we should adopt an accepting mindset. Even if we do not regret anything, we must accept it completely when we realize it is incorrect. "To do it unaware that it is improper; However, doing it knowingly is improper. Accepting it when someone mentions both will undoubtedly boost your self-confidence.

Emotional Maturity: Some individuals express whatever it is they are feeling; some do so through joy; some do so through anger; some cry for anything; some cry out of tension; some even get tired of the smallest thing; Self-Confident people do not worry about such things; instead, they make mature decisions and reject the idea that any decision made out of anger is wrong. When you make a serious decision without becoming dependent on rage or decaying into a coward, your confidence will be evident.

Ability to accurately assess our capabilities: The ability to ascertain our capacities is self-confidence. We must first trust ourselves ten times as much as we trust other people. Then and only then will we be able to recognize who we are. Each of us has a remarkable ability that allows us to assess our strengths and limitations. Your confidence will shine through when you make this ability known. Let me re-submit to you a few more poems that I have written about self-confidence.

The seed of self-confidence...

Let's start a search... Yes, the search for self-confidence!

I'm looking, I'm looking... I'm looking until dawn!

Missing, Yes not found... Missing in the eye!

In yesterday's storm... Like a dead grain of rice!

Like a stranded newcomer... Like a ruined Cuddalore!

The cane of self-confidence... The young man who is lost!

What if you're tired... How can you stand still?

Sow the seed of self-confidence!

All the seeds should come out!

All the seeds that come out should stand straight!

All the seeds should grow strong and strong!

All the strong seeds should ripen!

All ripe seeds should bear fruit!

What is the tsunami, what is Nisha!

No matter how many may come, we won't be afraid!

Make failures as Stepping Stones! Make successas fruitful!

The prosperity of our lives will increase!

To spread the fame of our country!

Come with me so that I can give you a shoulder! Join hands!

Let's get ready to Succeed!

Dear Readers and friends! I'm assuming you understand the meaning of self-realization, confidence, and self-confidence. The second approach we'll look at next is Time Management. Let us be ready to read, maintain, and manage our TIME.

❑

Chapter – 3
Time Management

Dear friends! Now it is time for us to look into the importance of Time Management. Three charming Tamil proverbs highlight the importance of time:"Kaalam Pon Pondrathu; Kadamai Kan Pondrathu" which means "Time is like Gold; Duty is like the Eye", "Kaatrulla Pothe Thootrikkol" which means "Sprinkle when there is wind"; "Kalathe Payir Sei" which means "Do everything in Time". Similar proverbs in english "Time isn't the main thing. It's the only thing." – said by Miles Davis. The famous inventer Benjamin Franklin quotes that "The lost time is never

found again". Also,We will discover in this chapter how crucial "time management" is to succeed in life.

Here, we'll look at how changing time effectively is vital to thrive in life, why it's not necessary to have a lot of time, and how crucial it is to practice good time management. Please come on.

The first thing to understand is that every human being value other people's time 100 times more than their own. Students' time is precious, like gold—it's like an eye. For this reason, if I am asked to speak as a special guest at any event, I always arrive fifteen minutes early and ask them to begin the performance. We are free to wait as long as we like, but I believe that the students shouldn't have to wait for us.

Some friends don't even have self-interest. His own time is unimportant to him. The other guy in particular doesn't give a damn about squandering time. A person who disregards time will not follow through on any action. "He is not fit for THAT. Who doesn't give importance for Time, will not fit for anything."

Maybe you've seen a few people. They are either in front of the TV or sitting on their hands and mobile phones at any given time. Time-pass, i.e., I'm seeking entertainment, if you ask. Indeed, it will squander your valuable time and cause a cut. A person's ability to remember others and even oneself may be impaired if they begin watching TV serials. This can waste your valuable time and ultimately impede your success.

I'm not arguing against watching TV for that purpose. See TV for a bit to give yourself a mental break. Observe the news. Once a week, watch a movie. It's not that I'm advocating against using your phone. If you spend your valuable time just for your needs, even your time will lead to success, and chances for success will present themselves to you unknowingly.

God who gave the gift:

Some of my friends and some of the kids look at me and ask this question. How do you manage to fit in all of this? You create songs, compose music, sing, rebuild musical instruments, write books, read books, make lots of inventions and innovations, assist others, teach students, play games, and more.

Then, I'm jokingly conveying a message. I had a dream one day where God spoke to me. Would you want a gift? he inquired.

I replied to God saying, "Oh God. You have given 24 hrs time for everyone.. If you could only give me 36 hours a day, I'd be content. In addition, God has granted me thirty-six hours a day." "Is that so!" they would ask.

"There is no such thing," I declared. Like everyone else, I only have twenty-four hours in a day. I can only accomplish this by practicing time management, effectively planning and using my time, and not wasting any time at all. We can prevail," I declare.

The majority of individuals are unaware of the importance of time. Some people show absolutely no respect. First and foremost, one must acknowledge that it is always too late—every day, every minute, every moment. Some people left the train in the span of two minutes and perished from a lack of access to medical care. You won't be allowed to write the exam if you leave home a little later than usual and miss the bus. Those who have left the fort also exist. Some people have also lost out on employment prospects as a result of a ten-minute wait. Some people have also lost out on life.

Rectification of punishment for wrong Doing:

Just 90 of the 100 people who could have won did so because they were delayed. However, they won't recognize that error. Error is inherent in human nature; yet, once an individual recognizes their error, they must take action to rectify it. There needs to be an attitude that nothing should be delayed going forward. We won't approach the fire once it has burned once. Likewise, we ought to take prompt action if a mistake has been made."The fool would have been dead. We must learn from what happens to others around us, according to the fact that "the wise man will see and repent".

In consideration of this, this section provides a thorough examination of the value of time, efficient time management techniques, and time management principles.

❑

Five Principles of Time Management

"You may delay, but time will not. That is, you may delay, but the past will not come back," is the admonition of Benjamin Franklin, a brilliant explorer.

Following these five fundamental guidelines can help you become a better time manager. Indeed, similar to the Panchsheel precepts. You complain that it seems like Ayyappan Sir won't give up the numbers, and I hear from your mind-voice.

By organizing yourself according to these principles, you'll be able to finish more work in less time. In other words, it is referred to as productivity, effectiveness, or efficiency in English. The following are the five key ideas of efficient time management:

- Planning and acting

- Determining priorities

- Setting realistic goals and timelines

- Avoiding distraction and lethargy

- Smart work instead of hard work

1. Planning and Executing:

As far as possible, the task you can accomplish each day should be planned on the first day. The assignments must be finished within the allotted time, so you must plan your work from the very first day and proceed accordingly. This includes deciding when and how long to spend on the projects you have selected.

To ensure that the task you undertake is done correctly, you must plan, prepare, and process it. The same is true of the 3P - plan, prepare, and perform as they are known in English.

I'm going to tell you a story to illustrate this. You'll get it cleared as soon as you give me the tale. Any age group will be enraged, regardless of how many times the tale is told. All right, may we now begin the story?

Ramu and Somu were two close friends who lived in a village. They are not educated. However, Somu would always be rude in his work and would not think at all, whereas Ramu was able to plan, research, and carry out anything he did. Despite this, both of them had a strong desire to work hard and make money.

They used to go into the forest together and chop down trees to make fuel. They used to break firewood every day and make money from it in a firewood shop in the village. 20 kg of firewood will earn you Rs 100 if you break it. At the very least, Ramu splits up to 100 kg of firewood per day. As a result, he made between Rs. 400 and Rs. 500 per day, although Somu could only split 50 to 60 kg of firewood in a day. Consequently, Somu was always paid less than Ramu, as he only made between Rs. 250 and Rs. 300 a day.

Somu doesn't know why this is the case. Regardless, we arrive around 9 a.m. with Ramu to split firewood. We split wood till five o'clock at night, but Ramu is the only one that makes a lot of money. How do you feel about that? He doubted his ability to cut more firewood, so one day he went to their employer and questioned, "What is it, Ramu and I come to work at the same time, we finish the work at the same time, but how can he cut more firewood?" The manager declared, "I know what. And Ramu is your friend! Ask him.

As he heard everything, Ramu turned to face Somu and revealed the work's secret. "I mean, Somu, I'll shave off my axe tonight if I have to break the firewood tomorrow. Using a worn-out axe to cut firewood takes a long time.

Likewise, you will nap and go to sleep right away after eating during the lunch break. I shall even then get my axe ready. I can cut more firewood because of one thing I do on purpose to cut down on the amount of time it takes to cut firewood."

Ever since Somu has also embraced the practice of prepping the axe before chopping firewood. Thus, his pay increased.

What friends! It is true that if I prepare and follow through, I will succeed. I have had a great deal of success in my life, and for that reason, I have succeeded. I hope you now see how crucial planning is to effective time management.

2. Determining priorities:

In Tamil, there is a lovely proverb. "Sprinkle it when there's wind." The cultivator discards the paddy beads in the drum after harvesting the crops and separating them from the straw. The paddy beads can be detached and taken out when it is blown or sprinkled. Is it possible to accomplish something more effectively in the absence of wind? When there is no breeze, can it be sprinkled? For this reason, the proverb "Sprinkle when there is air" refers to the need to seize favorable opportunities when they present themselves. Friends, do you know what I mean when I say this? Missing an opportunity leaves us uncertain about when or if we will receive another chance, as well as why.

Establishing your priorities, students, is the first step, in my opinion. In other words, during the study period, studying is the only thing that matters. It is the thing that students ought to prioritize. I'm not refusing to participate in your favorite activity, nor am I demanding that you put it on hold. Studying should come first; everything else may wait. Consider the scenario where you play cricket every day out of habit, but the next day you have an Exam, let us assume. Anytime is a good time to play cricket. But the exam won't happen until it does. This cannot wait. This is what they say: "Sprinkle when there is wind."

We will undoubtedly succeed if we prioritize all we do. Studying, putting in effort, believing in your abilities, achieving your goals, and experiencing achievement are all priorities. If you follow through on all of this, the discomfort will disappear and your objectives will become the focus and eventual realization.

This is the reason I advise giving your studies priority while studying, making sure not to give importance for movies, TV shows, weddings, or sporting events. With life, you can accomplish it."

What friends! You can only be successful in everything you chose to accomplish if you can prioritize your time effectively. Prioritize important urgent jobs first, then important but non-urgent work, then urgent but non-important work, and lastly, once you have planned and carried out duties that are neither urgent nor important, success will undoubtedly be on your side.

I hope you will see how crucial "setting priorities" is to time management if you want to succeed in life if you want to succeed if you want to ascend to the top of success.

3. Setting realistic goals and timelines:

Establishing objectives gives us a sense of motivation and encourages positive attitudes and actions. They help us live successful lives, pay attention, and work at a faster pace. Additionally, goal-setting enhances time management by encouraging a feeling of inner urgency when performing a task and satisfaction when it is finished.

Well-thought-out goals are an excellent tool for time management. By SMART, what do you mean? Shouldn't being smart be the aim when it comes to smart TVs and smartphones? What is that, SMART, then? You've probably encountered a lot of explanations of this word's usage in colloquialisms and on the Internet. Here, we'll take a slightly different approach to defining realistic aims.

SMART – Specific, Measurable, Achievable, Relevant, Time-Bound

Specific i.e., referential: to bea well-defined, clear, thoughtful, and honest goal.

Measurable means measurable: You need to be with specific criteria that measure your progress in achieving the goal.

Achievable, i.e., achievable: it must be a goal that can be easily achieved or achieved without complications, there is nothing impossible, but it must be a goal that is achieved by istapattu rather than achieving it with great difficulty.

Relevant i.e. touted: It should be a goal that is accessible, realistic, and relevant to your life's purpose.

Time-Bound i.e. Time Limit: The aim is to create a clearly defined timeline, including the start date and the destination date.

Realistic goals are an important component of time management. Once the goals have been set, it is easy to chart the path to achieve the goal and allocate the resources and time required to adhere to it.

In the same way, you have to give yourself a deadline or a time limit to do any work you perform within this range. That period needs to be reasonable; if I give myself an impossible deadline and expect to finish in three days what which ld take ten, I will fail miserably. I won't be able to complete the math classes that should take a week on the same day.

Simultaneously, it is necessary to estimate the duration required to complete this task. A reasonable timeline can then be established. You can only use that time efficiently after that.

It is crucial that you finish your assignment on time because any interruptions will also affect the duties that come after them.

4. Avoiding distraction and lethargy:

Planning is not a one-word solution; rather, it requires attention and good execution. The entire advantage is that, and many individuals make meticulous plans and schedules, but then cross the line when the moment comes.

The primary causes of this are tiredness and distraction. To complete tasks on time and with caution, you must first do the necessary job without becoming lethargic, and then, while working, you must not divert your attention from the task at hand. Achievement is also evident.

5. Smart work instead of hard work:

There are often two approaches we might take to our work. Labor-intensive labor is one; delicate labor is the other. In the fine labor mode, this is something we must become used to.

The essence of hard labor is doing things voluntarily, and we often participate in unrelated activities while working. Doing this will make us lethargic. A hard job requires no planning or preparation, takes a lot of time, wastes your valuable time, and is very expensive financially. This is a laborious task. The laborious task that the donkey bears as well.

But Smart Work is about planning, preparing the work for it, concentrating solely on the work, and completing it successfully. How to do that work can be done easily. We can prevent waste of time. "Hard work never fails. But Smart Work always triumphs" is a translation of the English proverb. Yes. Hard work Never Fails. Smart Work Ever Succeed. That is to say, there is no place for the word failure, it is always victory, the proverb says.

❏

Chapter – 4
Leadership Quality

The leader! Or Follower!

Everybody in the world aspires to be a leader in some capacity, such as the head. I'm not talking about the thalapathy or the Thala in the movies. In school, when you are put in a group and required to study, those four pupils become the group and grow to want to be the group leader. The ambition to lead a class as a student, or to become a class leader, is another. After that, everyone in the school will want to be a student leader or pupil leader.

As a college student, you aspire to be a nominee in an election, win favor from peers, and rise to the position of leader. After completing your education and starting a career, you will keep working toward becoming a union leader at your current place of employment. If your work or trade requires strong talents, you will be given managerial leadership responsibilities. Being a teacher allows you to become headmaster. You can become a chief scientist if you are a scientist.

Before entering politics, a person must rise to the position of village Chairman or president Subsequently, he was elected as MLA then, everyone will aspire to be a minister and eventually the chief minister. There will subsequently be aspirations to become prime minister. A man can't exist without a dream. Many people would rather be in charge than serve everyone. Yes. included me too.

Having the urge to "become a leader" is not a bad thing. Are we, however, qualified to hold a leadership position? That must be looked at first. If not, we must choose what kind of credentials to create. It is important to keep working to improve the requirements for the same.

Qualifications for Leader:

A few things can be mentioned explicitly, even if becoming a leader requires many qualifications. Based on my own experience, I can state that being a great leader requires possessing the qualities of being the leader of each letter in the word LEADER.

L - Listener or Loyal

E - Elegance

A - Awareness

D - Decisive

E - Ego-Less

R - Reachable

L: Loyalty or Listener. In other words, the letter L comes first in the term leader. There are two categories of qualifications: Loyal and Listener. You must, first and foremost, be a listener— that is, someone who pays attention to what others have to say. A positive impression is only formed when you pay close attention to what other people have to say. Your open and receptive mind will be exposed to it. The most effective leader may be the one that puts others or those who report to him first in his listening list. I think it is impossible for someone who dares to listen to others to be a leader, a regular servant, or even a human being.

L stands for loyal, which is faith or truth. A leader must also have the same level of faith in his followers as he does in his servants or those who work under him. He ought to have loyalty to the office that hired him and to the work he accomplishes. Thus, one needs to be genuine. The best leader may be him.

E - Elegance: There should be a sense of elegance in whatever you do. Being able to gently explain it to others and get them to accept it without defending our actions is a virtue. That adds yet another crucial requirement for becoming a leader. Rather than telling people they must follow my instructions, it is preferable to gently convince them to accept it. This trait is what will elevate you above others and turn the average person into a leader.

A - Awareness: I. "Does a person who does not know the present day of the town needs a position of leadership?" is one example of a colloquial statement. Says they. We must pay close attention to what is going on around us if we want to become better leaders and flourish in our roles. You ought to understand it completely. You need to read a lot and know a lot to do it. It's imperative that you maintain contact with experts in the field. You'll regress if you don't keep yourself prepared and current. Those that are behind you will take the lead and advance. As a result, awareness is crucial.

D – Decisive: Resolution. Being able to make judgments and being organized are essential qualities for a leader. Teams want guidance and a clear vision, which we can offer. we need to be prepared to make the necessary corrections if we realize we made a mistake.

E – Ecoless: We need to be "ego-less" as leaders. Leaders ought to be receptive to ideas and keep their egos in their wallets. Being humble is a quality that we should all possess.

R – Reachable: Our teams need us to be there for them. They ought to understand that you don't find it difficult to talk to them. Assure them that they can talk to you at any time and that you are available to them.

Don't BLAME OTHERS

Thus far, in addition to what was already mentioned, I believe that not placing blame on others is a crucial component of being a leader.

- Don't Put the BLAME on others.

The most common weak justification we hear is something like "Nothing's right here, except me." Others still claim that the content and the system are flawed. If everything is there, I'll make it great." "Saying that the street is crooked to someone who doesn't know how to dance" is how one could describe it. It was increasingly common to assign blame for his shortcomings to others.

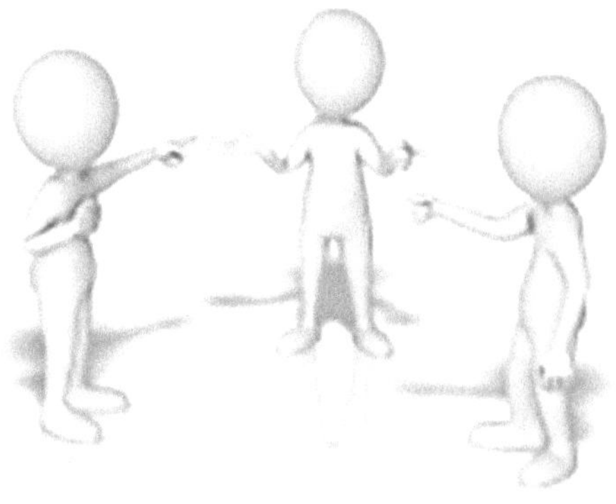

Let us assume, we are keep walking. On the way, we knock into the stone that is in front of us. "Stone kit me" is the most typical phrase we use when blood flows. It felt, for some reason, as though a stone had pursued him and struck him. Let's continue traveling along the route. Unaware that there might be a nail or thorn in the path, we would punch it. But you will be shocked by what we are going to say. How about "The thorn is punched"? What if the thorn finds us and punches us? We always want to blame other people in this way.

Say "It's not my fault" if something goes wrong with the work I'm doing. It's his fault," he stated, going on to say that the most significant barrier to becoming a leader would be the impracticality of finding a solution. If something goes wrong and you are the team leader, you should take the first fallout. Instead of blaming others, you need to consider how to fix the error.

The Missile Man, A.P.J., our former President of India, is an illustration of this. I want to tell you about an incident that happened in APJ Abdul Kalam's Life.

Leadership in Kalam's Life:

Dr A.P.J. Abdul Kalam oversaw the SLV-3 satellite launch project in 1979. Under Kalam's direction, over a hundred scientists collaborated with him as well. ISRO's chairman at the time was Professor Satish Dhawan. They were all employed on SLV-III, India's first satellite launch vehicle. The team as a whole was led by Dr. Satish Dhawan. Although it took a lot of labor and dedication to launch the SLV-3 satellite, the endeavor was a complete failure at the time.

This is how former Indian President Kalam described the incident to an audience at a television show in 2013. "The HLV-3 is a team of more than 1,000 workers who have been working tirelessly for a decade (ten years) and are working specially and are on standby at the launch pad," Kalam stated in describing the incident.

At the launch site, or launchpad, in Sriharikota, the countdown began. The computer halted the launch and displayed a warning message after the countdown. However, Kalam, the director of missions, had to consult with other specialists to make a judgment in such challenging circumstances. In other words, the angle inaccuracy is little. It was moreover guaranteed that the control equipment we possess might rectify it.

Later, after the system had gotten out of hand, the specialists, who had high hopes for the computations, counseled them to keep on. The launch pad's initial phase of operations was the best of its four phases. The launch's second structure wasn't operating correctly. This caused the satellite to enter the Bay of Bengal and settle there, avoiding the launched objective and departing from its required orbital location.

According to Dr. Kalam, the event was a botched first meeting. Everybody in the group has a puzzled expression on their faces. That was Kalam's first failure since he was unsure of how to handle the matter, react to the higher authorities, or explain the error that had occurred.

All the people in the group were depressed. Nobody even eats dinner correctly. Sleeping soundly is absent. That evening, Kalam got a call in the interim. "In response to the failed   event that occurred, a press conference, or press meet, has been scheduled. You have to answer and take part in it."

Kalam was unsure about what to do. They enquire quite a bit! You have squandered millions of rupees using tax revenue from the government. Who is going to be made to pay for this loss? How will you resolve this? There'll be inquiries. What plan do we have to meet it? What will be our course of action? Kalam was perplexed. He didn't sleep at all that night.

It felt like it always would be the morning as usual. Kalam arrived at the news conference with a confused heart. APJ Abdul Kalam's name board was displayed on a signboard in the middle of the dais. With trembling, Kalam went to the stage and slid into the designated seat. Seated beside him were other scientists. A panic of some sort.

There was a great deal of consternation during the press briefing when ISRO chairman Satish Dhawan came in a manner that no one had anticipated. Kalam approached and took a seat on the chair he was occupying. He requested that he bring Kalam an additional seat. However, what transpired next was amazing. "Keep everyone calm."I am spearheading this press conference myself," he declared, before continuing, "Please feel free to ask me any questions you may have."I'll respond to myself," Dhawan declared. The person in charge, Satish Dhawan, accepted full responsibility for the task's failure and all criticism.

"Let me start by congratulating the scientific team for their outstanding work on the HLV-3 project." I would have been successful in this endeavor if I had led this team appropriately. I accept whole accountability for this setback. He declared, "I am confident that next time they will be able to successfully achieve the goal they take up. I will always have the honor of leading a good, very good team."

The news conference came to an end. Dhavan made a call to the Kalam team. Why consider this to be a failure? Consider this as "FAIL - "First Attempt in Learning" "Remember that failure is the first step toward success and use this experience to learn the lessons you have learned from it." Indeed, you can. No one can do it if you can't. Keep believing that you can go forward and reach your next location. Without offering any consolation, ISRO Chairman Satish Dhawan declared, "The victory belongs to you." His gaze was locked on Kalam.

With confidence, everyone set out to tackle the next task. On July 18, 1980, the next year, Kalam took the initiative and encountered Rohini R. The S-1 was positioned and launched into space by Kalam's scientific team. Not only did Kalam celebrate the win, but so did all the other scientists. Everyone was having a very nice moment. It seemed as though I had been at night when I received a call. Yes. In press conference mode, that night, nobody slept at all. The fact that it's a victory is the cause. One celebration alone pleased everyone to content.

The morning dawned. All the participants arrived by eight o'clock for the nine o'clock event. Every face has an almost limitless joy on it. This time, the words "Satish Dhawan" were displayed in the center of the stage, while the words "Abdul Kalam" were displayed on the side. Everyone was anticipating the arrival of Satish Dhawan.

There was also Satish Dhawan. He took out the nameplate "Abdul Kalam" and put it in the center, moving the "Satish Dhawan" nameplate out of the way. Dhawan made him stand in front of the camera, in the light and identified as him, Kalam. "Kalam and his associates are the driving force behind this entire success. He said, "So Kalam ji will answer all your questions," and he got off the platform.

With that leadership quality, Satish Dhawan was the only person in Kalam's line of sight. Truly, that is "leadership"? It was a fantastic occasion that let the community realize how outstanding he is as a leader. He is well aware that the greatest attribute of a true leader is accepting responsibility for his defeat in the event of failure and sharing it with his allies in times of victory.

What friends! Are you following? You have to be aware of the essential skills needed to be a leader and to become one.

❑

Chapter – 5
Opinion and Conclusion

Go ahead, my friends! This chapter will teach us what difficulties need to be conquered to succeed. It is not a conclusion, but rather a series of talks on the subject of overcoming challenges. I will impart to you my knowledge on how to turn setbacks into learning opportunities, how to conduct successful experiments, how economics is not a barrier at all, and how success is certain if ignorance is eradicated and superstition is dispelled.

Failure is the first lesson. i.e. Use your initial setback as a teaching opportunity for future success. Make it a teaching moment. Don't make the same error when attempting again.

Failure is the first step to success. It won't go away at all if you give up and allow failure to force you to sit down. Failure will grab hold of you if it overwhelms you. Consequently, learn from every setback and use it to propel yourself up the success ladder. After that, you cannot fail.

If there is assurance, then success is guaranteed. Yes, comrades, in line with the poetry by the famous Tamil poet Bharathi, which states that one should have a firm mind, pleasant speech, a good memory, and the fulfillment of one's dreams. You do indeed succeed in life. Written by Soma Valliappan, "Only Determination" is a book that has been published. I become a author of many books, today as a result of reading such a books. Yes, it wouldn't be overstating things to suggest that the book served as a guide for me when I told you about my successes.

In the hopes that you can find some comfort in the quotes from some of the novels that I liked reading, I have included them here. May the world experience the same delight that I have.

Let's start a joyous journey: "Life is about going up step by step. Pleasure isn't just upstairs. There's every step of it too," says Wadley, a genius. Learn from rose to live with flowering amid thorns. Learn from the child to shed tears without sorrow. Those who do not change track are those who never stumble. Smile is the sacred language taught by flowers. The signs of success are smile, glow, composure, contentment, smile, and enthusiasm.

The secret to success: The attitude that good will happen, the determined goal, the habit of thinking correctly, self-discipline, going the honest way in everything, remembering the lesson of failure and moving forward, motivation, keeping the body and mind healthy, and taking time out. It is the secret of successful people to make the most of the opportunity as planned, to act with the same vigor, and to break the secret and to benefit many, imbibe these words in your subconscious mind without reading them at all. Success is for you, and so for us.

Faith is God: There should be no negative attitude and there should never be any inferiority complex. The Content is Important rather than the Container. Let us give difficulty to the suffering itself, and we must be afraid of ourselves. The only thing we have to fear is FEAR itself. Yesterday is empty time, tomorrow is the future, and today is the time of the hour.

Success if you bow down: If I can, it is self-confidence, if I alone can, it is the over confident, if I can, it is mistrust. If I have a head-weight, it cannot win. For example, the matchbox and the matchstick, just as a matchstick with a moment on its head, when it rubs against a matchbox, its head is burned to ashes and disappears, so those who have a head-weight can never win. If you have humility during success and courage during failure, success is certain.

The cause of success and failure: The reason for success can be anything you want. The main reason for failure is only four: shame, hesitation, fear, and ambiguity. Chase down failure. "I am a believer. Psychologists say that you have to say ten times a day, "I will win anything."Live while you are alive, do not die before you die, and chase away the spirit of failure.

Ready to achieve!: Decide what is important, be prepared to give up anything, and be honest. Inculcate in your mind the eight-letter mantra "I can do it". Instead of hard work, learn to work gracefully. Do SMART WORK rather than HARD WORK. Be the first, or be with the first, and the thought will be fulfilled If you have a dream and enthusiasm for it.

The key to success: If obstacles are broken, you can win. Economics does not matter. Beauty is not external, but within, in your thoughts. There is no age limit for learning and achieving, there is no distinction between caste, religion, men, and women, and there is no difference between urban, rural, government school, and convent school.

The secret of success: Break the laziness, make an effort, break down obstacles, and pluck the fruit of success. This is the secret of success.

My dear respected students! Please don't study just for marks. You have to grow up in this society as respectable woman and respected man, you have to rise in life. Don't study hard, study with interest, involvement dream of what you want to be, and read a lot of good and well-thought-out books to become good people, and rise in life.

In conclusion, Dear parents, teachers, students, friends, brothers, and sisters, consider reading a book as a respiratory duty and buy the best works, read it every day, let the habit of reading grow, let the growing generation prosper and win in life.

Every reader and student who reads this book should imbibe and feel the ideas expressed in this book. You have to achieve. It would not be an exaggeration to say that there are a lot of books that have turned me into an achiever who was normal. If you think that this book was a crutch and inspiration for you to realize yourself and to raise yourself in life when you once succeeded and stood tall, that is my happiness. I who have written the book will also be satisfied.

My dear friends, my dear dignified students, dear readers, wonderful teachers who are doing charity work! My heartfelt thanks to all of you, and once again, goodbye from you until I meet you on a good topic.

Your friend, People's Scientist
Dr G.S. Ayyappan

❑

www.ingramcontent.com/pod-product-compliance
Lightning Source LLC
LaVergne TN
LVHW041443170726
843492LV00008B/2780